GW00858658

Snowflake

Faysal Mikdadi

First published in 2013

Printed and distributed through www.lulu.com

Cover design and Author's photograph by Faysal Mikdadi

All rights reserved

© Faysal H Mikdadi

ISBN: 978-1-291-26944-4

Faysal H Mikdadi has asserted his right under the

Copyright, Designs and Patents Act, 1988 to be identified

as the author of this work.

All the characters in this book are fictitious, and any resemblance to

actual persons, living or dead, is entirely coincidental.

To all those who make the imaginary worlds of my stories

so real, especially Susan Walpole, Catherine Pattinson and

Richard Mikdadi

In deep appreciation and eternal gratitude

By the Same Author

Novels:

Chateaux en Palestine, Paris, France, 1982.

Tamra, London, United Kingdom, 1988.

Return, Raleigh NC, USA, 2008

Short Stories:

Christmas Stories, Raleigh NC, USA, 2012

The Dabawis and the Shargawis, Raleigh NC, USA, 2012

Poetry:

A Return: The Siege of Beirut, London, United Kingdom, 1983.

Painted into a Corner, Raleigh NC, USA, 2013

Bibliographies:

Gamal Abdel Nasser, Westport, USA, 1991

Margaret Thatcher, Westport, USA, 1993

Faysal Mikdadi, Born in Palestine in 1948, was carried to Lebanon where he was brought up and was given his rather unsuccessful education. He moved to Britain in 1967 and has lived there since. He is an English Literature specialist with a keen interest in the Nineteenth Century Victorian novel and in Shakespeare. His published works include novels, poems, short stories, bibliographies, educational essays and regular contributions on current affairs.

He started writing at a very early age during a turbulent and unhappy childhood. His urge to write comes from a deeply felt need to try to make sense of a disordered and crazy world and to laugh at his own rather stodgy attitudes to a much sought after quiet life. It also comes from his need to laugh at others' predictable higgledy piggledy existence and to celebrate his deep love of nature – the only place in which he sees any order and a semblance of logic.

These two stories were written during a midwinter visit to Nouchâtel, Switzworland and an oqually ovooativo autumn vioit to Florence, Italy. They should speak for themselves, showing the author trying to make order out of chaos.

Contents

Snowflake   9

Piazza della Repubblica   81

Snowflake

A Journey in Time

A snowflake fortunately does not recognise its limited
lifespan
And the eternal cat sat on the mat.

Life is a crossword puzzle: cryptic but satisfying even
unresolved.

The rag doll sits, shot away, wondering where the wall is;
And on either side of the high wall
Stands a man wondering what is on the other side.

Old age is the other end of its young self
Only the young one doesn't see it.
And the old one confusedly regrets
All the missed opportunities of its sister self.

Endless images flutter by each
As inconsequential as a snowflake

Who is a private long living soon to die individual.

Alcohol dulls the pain that hurls abuse at those most loved,
And refuses the opportunities soon to be missed.

I'm the conscience of my own universal people forged in
the smitty of their Irish wombs.

Many loves merging into one point at fifty
And poured into a last lasting love.

Telling the future is bad for you
It sucks abuse from the unbelieving
And sinks your heart to ageing aches.

A different time line allows
The done undone
The possible impossible.
And makes you laugh at the disordered existence of
squeamish flies feeding off excrement.
And your parents do mess you up my child.
With their frozen lives unshakeable.

Each image crystallised in the void of a soul

Until, full, it seeks lightness on the water

With imagined loves and loved images.

Lebanon's river of blood was made incarnadine by Adonis

spilling his life

Gored by a jealous boar in the slopes of milky mountains.

And yes, *dear reader*, it is the same world

You love in and others have died in.

As intended.

Being Palestinian, I am now found.

My Jerusalem is in these lines

Like my love, forever there.

I know I have brains but can't remember where I've put

them.

And Babushka laughs at her own old age

And tells all not to grieve.

I wish I could find a woman to undress

My soul.

I wish I could find a woman to unlock

My mind

And free it of all images

Except her face.

Ageless in love.

With an eye for the words of fiction.

And we will make love

Giving birth to healthy stories

Which will grow and continue our line.

Our words.

Our children.

Making order out of our chaos.

Neuchâtel, January in recent times

22.01

8.45 pm local time

It is like a journey in time.

The snow was friendly and welcoming. Within, my soul fluttered wavering like a snowflake not recognising its limited lifespan.

I saw the black cat still dormant. The Ingénieur Agricole, my dead father, still refusing to leave.

Then I saw her.

She looked confused to see me. Her hand shook as we engaged in polite conversation.

"I'm sorry. I'd forgotten you were coming."

I laughed and reassured her. Crossword puzzles littered her seat. Many completed. I thought of palindromes and spoke of my family.

"That stepson of yours is very intelligent, you know."

I nodded.

"You have the key. Unlock his inner self."

Not as senile as you appear. You have seen it. And no one is going to unlock anything. His mother has put a new lock in and thrown away the key: turning him into a rag doll.

9.15 pm

We sat silently. She repeated that she had forgotten that I was coming. Pointing to her head, she rotated her hand and said, "It's all jumbled up now."

Another silence.

"I will be eight this year. I mean ninety. I was born in eight."

I said that she looked well which she did not.

She smiled.

"You speak beautiful French. That's good."

I laughed too loudly and noisily recrossed my legs.

"I had forgotten you were coming."

The hand shaking uncontrollably. I thought of my wife and wished that she were there. I was an intruder on toothless old age. The old beauty still lurked somewhere behind the tired face.

"You need to go to town now."

I got up and followed her to the old bedroom. She switched all the lights on and showed me the bed, the bathroom, the towels and some books by my bed. I said thank you.

"I must go to bed now. I sleep late in the morning. Practice for the long sleep."

We laughed.

"You love your wife very much. Good. You must be patient. Let your passions rest. Very bright boy. You've always been very bright. Very bright. Stubborn but laughing. Bonne nuit. Keep laughing. À demain. We will eat filets de pèrche at Auvernier."

I drove into town. On the left. Dreaming. Going down a one-way street and thinking of what had gone wrong. First

Oxford. Now this. I sank into a depression and fought it. Images raced endlessly and I sat back. To watch. And relax.

I ate at the Touring. Filets de pèrche and a line of images.

I so wanted to speak to Paula.

But some inner turmoils are padded cells. Solitary confinements. Cold. Frigid. Impersonal. In need of confrontation.

And I am stubborn. Bright but stubborn.

I wish my days were connected each to each without end and *by natural piety*. The images said that they were. I sat by the lake for hours. Shivering and warm. In love with those images.

Or was it minutes?

"Merci monsieur. Bon apetit monsieur."

Still so ineffably polite and pleasant. Like a cottage kitchen with a cottage wife and a cottage fire.

Baby's friend still sat by the bar. Smoking. Her breasts warm and young. Her mouth bored. Her eyes still green. And she complained of hard work. Wished a rich Sicilian Jew would save her little life. Seek warmth, poetry and life in her small pointed breasts. And I thought sadly of how beautiful I thought my wife was. How warm and inviting. How she takes my manhood and voids my soul with her supplicating tiny eyes.

And cried for hatred of that damned, damning and damnable alcohol.

Thought of its Arabic roots and wanted her tilting head in my arms as we watched moving images.

"Al-co-hooool. My nephew. It's bad. Nuncle."

23.01

4.00 am

I returned to my stepmother's apartment and phoned Paula. I whispered about the luxurious seat on the aeroplane and the huge hired car. I felt a childlike pride. People like my innocence not so innocent and give me things. I did not tell her about that floating being in fur. Snowflakes gently touched her fur and glistened like dew on a morning rose. Blue.

"Are you American, monsieur?"

"No. British."

"Je suis Anne. And you, monsieur?"

"I'm sorry to appear rude but I wish to be alone, please."

"Pardon, monsiour." And she walks off. Talks to baby's friend whilst I feel pangs of guilt. She returns.

"Monsieur Mikdadi. I knew your papa."

I am interested. I think maybe that fur coat was the money we have been looking for. Maybe he – I hope that he – had her: breast in one hand and *The Kama Sutra* in the other. No *The Perfumed Garden*. I thought of Frank carrying *Fanny Hill* to Annie's to read to her. And Annie obliged. Like Fatimah. Ursula. Alison. And so many pebbles crunching their way into my fractured conscience. I am the conscience of my people forged in the smithy (pronounced smitty) of their Irish wombs.

"Monsieur, I was his nurse. You are so like him. Distingué. Un vrai gentleman."

I leave and phone Paula. A vrai gentleman my little smelly foot. Ask mia moglie, ma chère infirmière. I like words that rhyme. In time.

I could not face an empty bed and *Fugitive Pieces*. So I drove back into town in search of wandering Palestinian Jews' ghosts. And spent five freezing hours watching endless images.

And realised that my days were connected one to the other in prophetic joints and a never ending story.

Hugo rearranged his life in code. I shall try to be more honest and rearrange mine in images.

Each leaf spread its gentle barely visible veins telling our story. Daffodils swayed and excited us. She leant against a tree and undressed. I dreamt of the eternal epic and looked for poems. Collected yellow headed poetry and spread it on her body as it lay, nakedly arched, on wet grass. And after we finished the daffodils were crushed. Some stuck to us and laughed with us. She cried over her lost childhood and I wrote another poem. A sonnet to her.

She took me to St Mary's and I thought of Oxford in the Middle Ages. I read her Chaucer in Middle English and she laughed at my literary pretentions.

At the literary society I sat worshipping at my own feet. Talking of Hesse, Joyce and Lawrence. As the clock reverberated too long she said to take her from behind while she read *Bleak House*. The other one liked to pretend rape and I would not oblige.

I first saw her from my window.

"Forget it," said my Catholic friend, his conscience bulging with out-of-wedlock paternity. "She was made in paradise and is not for sinners like us."

I laughed and reminded him of my Muslim Paradise: running with milk and honey, green oases with Houris for the having.

"And what happens to women in your Paradise, then?" he asked mockingly.

But I was too young to care about the other half of the human race. How I loathed the brotherly half with beer sodden coffins: coffins made of wooden ignorance, solid chested prejudice and screwed down by a soulless presence that, like the dead, sees no past and no future.

My father was angry.

"Son, you talk garbage. Why on earth do you say that Beirut will be destroyed? A ball of raging fire? An inferno? Poetry, my boy, is all very well. But you know nothing of politics."

So I wrote my eleven page 1974 testament and begged my umbilical conformists to leave the city and my father would not speak to me eye to eye for five years. Until tens of thousands had died. Even then, he shook with anger when I forecast worse to come.

"This is our holocaust, Baba."

And he dismissed my words with a backward flex of his scarred hand.

And today I can see.

Cassandra's twin brother crushed by popular deafness.

Now I have learnt to bite my tired tongue.

My son laughed and said, "Hey dad, don't tell me I'm going to die. Because if you do, I shall go to bed, curl up and die. Might as well, Nostradamus!"

I ached to tell him that these were not prophecies. They were scientific, dialectic, repetitive historicity. You ape God and you will fall. You lie and you will be trapped. You give up and you will die. You reject consequences and they will gnaw at your inside like cancer. You play all the time and you will be nothing. Nothing.

I remembered Walid by the lake. Small shoulders and an oversized head telling me that if he lived to be eleven he will never understand "womans". I laughed and hugged him.

With my hands on his little – oh so little shoulders - I knelt before him sitting on the green bench. He looked at me with those big and, at times, old and wise eyes.

"Walid. There are possibilities inside you. Secrets. You carry the accretion of thousands of years of wisdom in every gene that you are made of. The secret of life is to achieve that curious state and to look for the answer. And when you begin to find it – for you will never find it fully – your landscape will become three-dimensional. Through poetry, music, literature, science – especially physics -, philosophy and love, then you will touch the face of God."

He nodded for so long that I thought that he had fallen asleep. He looked up at me suddenly.

"Daddy, like the flowers, the apple blossoms, Barney the donkey and your stories. Isn't it?"

I knew then that he would be an independent universal man. And I knew that Alison would be an independent universal woman when she compared the full moon to my Dream Bubbles and clapped her hands.

My marriage to their mother ended in 1979. The 11 February 1979 on the frontroom floor in Haughley. I looked in her eyes and I knew that something had died. Soon after that she moved to another world and her children looked confused and clung to me for years to come. I found her in a foetal heap in Warrender Terrace and panicked at her changing states. It frightened me.

"She's always been a little odd, my little girl. Look after her."

And the doctor had tea with us and smiled through his distinguished moustache and kindly eyes.

"Mild Schizophrenia, I should say."

I was surprised by the matter of fact diagnosis. Like a mild headache or cold.

And I was lost in a sea of multiplicity.

"Take me on the table with the bottle of Ketchup looking on."

She screamed contorting her face into a look of terror filled agony. And I wanted out.

I tried not to cry over the phone to my father. He told me not to ring him so often to check up on him. He said that I must get on with my life and not think about him. Then he sang me his Turkish song and swore at me in Turkish. Like he did at Jamal the Butcher in 1917 and hid in the tree while his mother entertained the murderous general. Later, she found her son and slapped him for his naïve nationalism. He loved telling me that story.

We talked literature, politics and Jewish humour. I, in my eclectic ill disciplined way. She, with her Irish lilt and melodious anglecisations. Like a gentle flower floating down the river of my dreams. Karina of my fertile soil. She never seemed to walk. Floated. We ate stale bread, listened to Mozart and made up little worlds. Dream bubbles that floated upwards and reflected a colourful sun until they burst.

Their mother burst them as we joined hands and danced in a circle. Alison laughing and Walid singing.

"I wish you were my mummy."

And I got angry and told him that he had a wonderful mummy of his very own.

Alison cried and said that mummy hugged her hard and pushed her off. Hit her so hard that her nose bled.

"Mummy hits herself at night, daddy. Against the wall."

And I remembered finding her sitting naked and masturbating, screaming my name as if it were some demonic chant.

My sister recently said that I really had had too much shit in my life. Enough was enough.

My brother laughed and told me that I married a loose screw. Dry and humourless. He looked at me and tilted his head, wincing at the pain in his foot.

"Maybe your writings are those of a genius. I think they are. I don't like'em though. Too much prick and not enough spunk. Say it as it is, not as it ought to be. And when you say it as it is; say it as it ought to be. Enough shit. Divorce your wife and marry our hostess."

He told me that during the night, she had entered my room and sat in the armchair watching me. She covered me up and kissed my forehead.

I had a vague remembrance of it but I had thought that it was a dream.

"Did you...?"
"No!" I replied angrily booauoc I wantcd to.
"Hmmm. This fidelity is a load of crap. Take the advice of a dying breed."

I laughed because I did not know then that he meant it. In the background Jessie Jackson was chanting "Keep hope alive" to an ecstatic crowd.

And the American people got the president that they deserved.

A year later I met Paula. And I had to wait for six years for her and I to marry and a hundred years of solitude for her to love me – the inner me. The real me.

And I fell in love with her.

Say it as it is. Not as it should be.

As it is: I love her.

As it should be: I don't want to say it, nuncle. I know the word. It is good for you in moderation.

I am not blind though I wish to be.

The images oppress me: Father on the verge of tears as I raise my voice.

Mother laughing at my definition of God as like air meaning everywhere. "Like air: like nothing" she giggled blowing smoke through her severe nose.

My sister hitting me for asking when my dead mummy will come back. A mere child herself thrust into the position of early motherhood by a stupid father who meant well.

My brother laughing and strapping my bloodied leg and saying that this was a cowboys and Indians game and that I was a hero. Not everybody got hurt in a bomb explosion.

My father talking to the doctor in English and the doctor telling him that I might die. I wanted to do my Elementary Certificate so that I could go to a public school. I cried.

My white shorts, my white socks and my white shoes. Aunt waving proudly as the Prime Minister gave me my rolled

Certificate with a red ribbon gloriously emblazoned "with distinction".

Four years later I was a revolutionary bum cunningly dodging bullets and being drenched in red dye. We occupied the United Nations building thinking it was the American Embassy and got beaten up.

Images of our little circle in the blacked out city. We sat on the roof of Marwan's house and threw bottles at the police.

Nasser was our hero.

Israel our holocaust.

Of those on the roof three have since died violently in Beirut.

Images of Fatimah.

"I love you, my prince. Your eyes shine."

I walked from Jerusalem to Bethlehem in search of her.

My father's unexpected admiration at "my courage" in defying the blackout and the curfew to find my beloved.

Tortured. Raped. Her vagina cut to shreds.

"Your eyes shine. And Bosnia will, one day, be Muslim"

Thirty years later.

She too, was Cassandra like.

I have never seen so much blood and skin. I hoped that she had killed the bitch who did this to her.

And she went home to Saudi Arabia: eternally childless and loveless.

Images upon images because of a few hours in Neuchâtel.

Like *Beirut Revisited*.

By candlelight, in the boiling heat of the day and the freezing lonely cold of the night.

We used to make up palindromes and Marwan suggested "eyeless in Gaza" and we laughed at his loveable blindness and ignorance and he laughed with us.

Thirty years later, I met Paula again and we married.

Hers was the last kiss, the last love, the last specialness. A true soulmate. She so vulnerable and I so childlike. Refusing to grow up. Like pulling teeth out.

It is her softness I love. Her tears at a soppy movie. Her smile. Her surprise at the ordinary. Her love of beauty and order. Everything in its place. And I know what the problem is and dare not tell her. The alcohol is an anaesthetic. Like the cigarettes and the food.

Yet I love Paula – my own Paula. Will never hurt her. Will never abandon her. Will never deceive her. Will always love, cherish and protect her. If only she would let me instead of carrying her interminable hurts which came before me. I am not blind. I see it as it is. Not as it should – ought to – be. All these images have, for now, cleansed my aching soul. Mended my fractured conscience.

I just want my eternal beloved to be happy. Satisfied with what is. NOT what might have been.

All the tears of Ashtaruth will not wash the bloodied gore of yesteryears.

Paula can give up her alcohol. She can trust her son's natural and real love for her without stifling his intelligence and potential achievement. She can trust her family with all the truths of our disordered lives. And let herself be eternally loved, cared for, cherished and laughed with.

Mine is an innocent – though at times angry – intelligence.

I lied to her and told her that my IQ was 149 and she called me an "arrogant boring old fart".

For 149 and a conviction she lets rip at me at regular intervals.

What would she do with 180 and a passion? Divorce me, probably. Yet, I love her every day. As I get more frightened of upsetting or angering her, I go quieter and say little for fear of allowing that passion to rant and rave.

What is it John Fowles wrote of me?

"An impossible man to live with. But his books make it worthwhile."

I felt so proud when I read that. Ten years ago almost to the day.

This morning and last night – rather yesterday morning and the night before – I so wanted her so – so special permission to be myself. Her "I'm here darling". Her "good boy" and "make a house" and "good night, sweetheart". Why be so frightened to ask?

For fear of losing her and her fear of my betrayal.

Good God! We have brought baggage from previous lives.

But I shall never ever betray my darling Paula. My wife.

Not a first love, but last. And last loves last until the last breath. Beyond this life will Paula live in my love drenched lines. I have the trust. And I want her trust.

The images became all of Paula. No words could describe the warmth of such images. The beauty of her very being.

Paula, you will lose nothing for loving in return for being loved. Come to me as you really are – with no need for anaesthetics of any kind.

I will always be there – even if it took *one hundred years of solitude*. Paula. Not Jenny.

It is morning now. Snow is still falling. And I am cold. So cold outside. Warm within. I will make a house and call your name softly. Good night.

10.00 am

Those few hours of sleep refreshed me as if they were endless days. Dried stale bread, buttered and helped along with sweet strong black tea.

She shook hands with me this morning. She asked about Alee-son. Wal-eed and Pa-aul. After Colette who still writes to her. After Pau-laa who was so gentille and made me so heureux.

At each answer she made notes in a diary.

"I write or I forget."

She wrote in large rounded letters.

"Paula is very nice. She is teaching little ones. Alison is talented in languages. Walid is at University in Wales's capital. Paul is clever but behind."

She suddenly looked up at me as if I had just appeared.

"What do you do now?" and her emphasis on the 'you' made me smile.

I explained and she got up to make a phone call.

I excused myself and went into town. Last I saw her she had a drawer on her lap and she rummaged through it.

I wandered what memory she was in search of. If only it were that easy. Write it down and you can forget all about it.

I went to Payot and bought *L'amour de loin*. An appropriate supplement to my easing soul.

Time does not make you forget. It grows and envelops you with memories. It does not oppress you with regrets but delights you with images of the then in the now. So beautiful. Not fully recognisable but still comforting.

Like the heat of Beirut fanned by the ice of Sanine on a humid afternoon. All those dreams imaged in our conscience – collective and immutable.

Across my table sits Henry Miller speaking in bad French. *Sexus*, *Plexus* and *Nexus*. And I now understand the need for those endless stories. Food for the soul: to fatten it for a Paradise that had died in Phnom Penh in April 1975 and every year before and since.

Oxford dreams of the real world telling its own story. I saw Irene standing on her balcony. In thirty years she has grown but not changed. I wanted to ask her about that bewitching hour in 1968. And realised how little I now understood but how much I truly appreciated and accepted.

My stepmother and I will have lunch at Auvernier – like the old old days.

How I hate those cords that break so easily. A trust: a plunge.

"Buy my sister a good car." And you, my dearest bitch, buy your brother some support in his hour of need. Your father some dignity in his loneliness. And your husband a job he likes and a workshop.

"My son. Before you remove that minute splinter in my eye, remove that fucking huge pole that blinds you so."

I feel proud of my two children surging ahead with laughter and disrespect in their hearts. Renaissance people. As intended.

3.00 pm

Ah! The Swissticality of it all. The very precision of their borrowed language with the stress on the so obvious. My brothers and sister hated this precision because of our inherent Lebanese aloof disorganisation. Our very perfection, immortality and leonine existence causes us to triumph over each and every conquering civilising mission. Who needs civilising when they are so perfect?

We had lunch at Auvernier. My dear stepmother was talkative.

"When I die, if ne faut pas être triste. I have had sufficient."

She said it exactly the same way that she did when she puched her plateful of fich towards me.

"I no longer have many teeth. I have had sufficient. Finish it off."

I did. We drank unfiltered wine. Cloudy and pungent it left a heavy aftertaste – like a chat with an angry Alison, a tipsy Walid and a drunk Paula.

"My son is good to me. He visits occasionally."

I nodded. Even a mother's old age is like a cuckoo clock. So precise. Unpossessive and undemanding.

I found her immersed in paper on my return after my morning in town. She threw a large sheet on the table.

"In the event of my death". As if choice were ours. "In the event of…"

I walked out on to the small balcony. All my father's plants had died. A small one struggled in the cold and I rubbed a minute leaf and smelt my fingers.

Thyme.

And Lebanon was in me. Hot. Cold. Rainy and thyme fragranced. I was little again. Hunting for eggs painted the night before. My kindly frightened sister encouraging us to be creative. So – so young. Too young to be a surrogate mother to two orphaned boys.

How that child ever grew into manhood is as deep a mystery as Swiss Cottagism. So impeccably polite and predictable.

I dozed by the lake.

Being Palestinian, I woke in blistering heat on an isolated beach. My Rose and I lived in a small but comfortable hut. We spent our evenings reading or writing. She sat across our large table, her glasses on her forehead writing poems on Jerusalem and its history.

"Imagine," she said. "Imagine if the Jews had succeeded in creating their Israel. We would not be here."

I laughed at such a bizarre notion. The very thought of not being Palestinian in Palestine.

We ate olives and strong bread. Drank local wine. And made love.

As we coupled and I looked into her eyes, I thought of what she had said. Those poor Palestinian Jews thrown out with the immigrants. They are scattered across the face of the earth making the best of exile and haunting our national consciences.

She looked at me and mouthed something. I knew. My soul poured away and we lay still – sweat from the afternoon heat steaming.

Late afternoon and our ageing neighbour, Yassir Arafat, called. He was excited showing us his new poetry book – just published. A thin volume with white yellowing sheets. On them were words – musical notes that only he could play.

Rosie told him of occupied Palestine. The Jewish State. He threw his head back and laughed.

"What a wonderful notion. I would probably be a little terrorist like that ageing bum Guevara in the jungles of Bolivia. The poor sod has been fighting American imperialism for thirty years."

"And what would I be?" I asked apprehensively as if this were for real.

"Oh, some crappy academic like a Sicilian Jew out of Palermo. Somewhere in the United States without Rose. And Rose would be an itinerant Arab wandering the land of Israel."

"No," said Rose smiling. "I couldn't live without my Anthony." She lisped the 'th' in Anthony so childishly.

I wanted to tell her that my name was not Anthony. It was Samir.

I did not want to wake up though.

Yassir lit a pipe. It smelt good. I wanted him to go so that I could go to bed with Rosie. Please.

Before I wake up.

We sat up in bed and read *Paul et Virginie* aloud. It was cold. We hugged and fell asleep. I froze and woke up shaking and shivering. Palestinian voices floated out of me. Children playing and laughing.

Go back to your own time line.

I did. In Neuchâtel and bought the stepone a bunch of red tulips.

I wonder where Rose is now. Wandering the land of our fathers? In search of the impossible. *Paul et Virginie*. Find the key to your heart. There are infinite possibilities. I miss Paula – my Virginie. So warm. Come to my silent worlds.

5.00 pm

Michaela entwined her arm through mine and said in all her 25 years of wisdom: "I don't know what the soul is. But I imagine that somehow our bodies surround what has always been."

"Your body does," I said mischievously. "But my dear, you're 25 years too late. I'm very happy to see you." I love you Akhmatova.

She bared her shoulder and it was old. And I would not kiss it.

My stepmother smoked two cigarettes in succession, doing her crossword puzzle. Her breathing was heavy. With a rattle in it.

I shall sleep by the lake tonight. At least my nights are connected one to one in piety.

"I am," he said proudly, "impervious".

8.00 pm

What an outrageous allegation! Paula claims – alleges –
that I embellish – lie. I do not my pretty little headed moglie.
I see fantastical connections between those things that are
not related. Fanciful and undulatingly foreign: like the rays
of the sun through white drapes swaying floating dust
sperms shooting out of my teenage vitals.

And tonight? Is this embellishment?

My stepmother laid the table, moved in the kitchen, and sat
down at five. I read. At six, I had a cigarette and smiled at
her. Feeling that the smile was sufficient conversation, I
returned to my book. At seven there was a smell of heat.
The oven was on with nothing in it. I told her. She asked
me to switch it off.

7.30. I was called to table. Like a condemned man to his
last call, I opened the window ajar for a chance of escape.
If the fish could not go that way, then I would.

"Special wine," she exclaimed.

I open the window a little wider.

No dinner. A steaming empty container.

"I forgot!" she said quietly.

A last minute reprieve to a life with hard guilt. Anyhow, the fish would have been in the oven for two hours!

I made a quick exit to have my third filets de pèrche in twenty hours.

Embellish my foot.

I phonod Paula tonight and wantod hor oo. Till ohc ɔɑid, "All fat and…" and I sensed sadness overwhelm me.

Love at a distance.

If only she would accept it as it is…

24.01

3.00 am

It is impossible to sleep. And I can not get Paula out of my head, my body, my hair and my soul. I think it an imposition to seek permission by phone so early in the morning. It is not the same, anyhow. No "I'm heres" to soothe an unbelieving soul.

I sat by the lake listening to the silence.

Each son or daughter should be legally required to visit an agèd P. It is the only chance to retreat. To reflect.

And it is so difficult not to.

I liked Paul's name for the stepone: Babushka. As a childish mistake, it would be sweet though some five years too late. As a semi-sarcastic comment it would be spectacular. A liberation for the boy at last.

"I do wish my mum and my aunt would stop hugging me like some three year old. Can't they see I don't like it? I tried to tell mum on Sunday but she looked so hurt. I can't. I know myself: I am too lazy and I can't be bothered – I wanted to say fucked…" And he carried the bags of food jovially prattling on about his plans. He wanted to do well but "knows" that he "won't". Can't understand why.

"Only you really listen. I like it when you say "crap, my boy" because I know it is".

"No one tells me what the psychologist says. I know I've got brains. Where have I put'em?" And we laughed as he leant against me.

"These are special times. Like our boys' weekends." Yes, they are. It is a pleasure to see a child grow, mature and make little mistakes. It is even a pleasure to see a child stumble on the highway of life, fall over, look around and decide to laugh at the pebble that tripped him. Up he gets and runs harder. Knowing that each fall maketh the man.

Behind the high wall I stand staring at is probably another man wondering what is behind the high wall he stands staring at. In my Palestine, houses are very white. Roofs low and flat. Inside they are cool with a gentle breeze. The streets outside are covered in red soil – shifting sands. I come home from my school. Villagers wave and hail: I write their letters and teach their children. Every time a child picks a book, I smile and say, squinting: "You are like Columbus. On the threshold of a New World. Read the book and you will grow to fit your soul."

And the soul being there waiting for its body to make the half. The half sheathed in love finds the whole.

I teach my children to love literature, art, music and imagination. I reward the curious and punish the idle and blind. But they are all curious.

It is not only knowledge I try to impart but also a real curiosity to ask why. To find out and express the findings.

I reach my home and walk in. The frontroom is littered with the untidy relics of learning. Pieces of cloth with colourful intricate Palestinian patterns for cushions. Music sheets with improvised words in childish handwriting. A book of poetry by Adonis and Darwish and the little known anglicised exile; that sad fool Mikdadi. Even a sponge squeezed enough times will produce pretty patterns. A Longman's English novel. And magazines.

My wife comes in and sees me. I smile my greeting and she strokes my cheek with the back of my hand. I turn it over to hers and kiss her brow.

Six children come in: laughing, bickering and never standing still. I pick the youngest up and hold several hands beneath. Nadia plays the lute and we listen.

After dinner, I tell them the story of their ancestors in Ottoman days. They listen intently and scream at Jamal the Butcher. Laugh at the British officer with his swagger and cry for the Jewish immigrants shot on the beaches.

At night, I read by my bed. A poem by Saroyan the Armenian baker: *Love at a Distance*.

I shed a cathartic tear and read it to my wife. She explains that line about the high wall and I undress. We sleep into each other and hope to wake later to prolong the pleasure. And we do.

My wife laughs and says that my little school will never close because we will people it with our love. We kiss.

And nine months later, I tell the Mukhtar that a new pupil in the girls' class will be starting school in four years.

"This is Chaplin, sir. Isn't it?" asks Leila angrily holding a European history book up high.

"No Leila, it isn't Chaplin. Looks like him though my dear. No. This was a man called Adolf Hitler who tried to rule Germany. He had some extreme views. No one took him seriously though. He died in a plane crash in 1930. Some people think that he might have become Chancellor but I doubt it. The German people are too intelligent for that. We know that from our Goethe, don't we?"

Half the class say yes and the other half say no and I laugh. We read a few translated lines from Faust. In my bad German, I give them a few others.

I believe in learning. Each of my children will soak in learning through their spongelike curiosity. And this way Palestine will live forevermore.

We teach Hebrew in my school. Minority languages are important. Under those odious British we had to teach English.

We called our little school Cardiff College and they were flattered the pompous imperialist fools. They could not see the insulting reference to culture murder.

And time for bed.

In Neuchâtel, Switzerland. Exiled bodies. Exiled hearts loving at a distance. Exiled souls whose only home is a candle flame. Attractively fatal.

You must see my family? Paula?

Time crawls so but hurtles by without a fourth dimension.

Take me to Oxford my little Palestinian buggy handler. Give your horse food and hay. My wife Omar waits and his finger, *having writ, moves on*. Good night, ma belle.

"Aid's pernicious," he screamed watching red noses all around.

"So is AIDS, *mon semblable, mon frère, mon hypocrite!*" I replied laughing.

"Clasp the alphabet to your heart, though there are tears in every letter."

Because learning liberates and breaks every shackling fetter.

Strive to know more, understand and explain how you become better.

Joining your days to those before you and all after you.

For you will never die.

Ever. My son.

5.30 am

Still can not sleep. Coffee sodden and cigarette poisoned I begin to hear noises. Until I realise that it is that lunatic downstairs arguing with thin air. Probably my light is irritating her. Strange how some people can not sleep for the sleeplessness of others. I ate a bowlful of Tourmmos on the balcony in my shorts. It was minus eight degrees but so wonderfully stimulating.

I heard jackbooted marching accompanied by shouts of "achtung" and "arbeit maken frei" and realised that Palestine was but a dream. Mary, with her black hair circling her pillow but a mirage. And our class full of children thirsting for learning a cloud with a silver lining: soon dissipated.

I saw the towering barometer and found out that Hussein could have never reached it. It had a metal fence around it. I climbed the fence and tried to give it a gentle knock. I could not. It felt awfully undignified and I tripped grazing my shin. That little detail made a mockery of my fiction. And I felt old. I was my father shuffling by the lake. Breathing heavily and muttering to myself.

I wish I could find a woman to undress

My soul and let my body cleanse its age.

I wish I could find a woman to unlock

My spirit and give it its old innocence.

But the more time passes…

I had endless coffees at the Touring and finished another book. I spoke to Paula by the lake and we planned to go to Lampedusa in Sicily.

Why do authors press so hard on mistakes? To obliterate them as if they never were?

But the more time passes

The more the crushing weight of experience

Of wrongs done and cruelties uttered

Bend a spirit down and over

To flip it upwardly

Towards heavenly dreams.

Creating moving images.

Each tattooed on a million cells

Fusing into our children's tomorrow.

My children. If you live to my age – almost half a century now. If you do: remember the funny precepts. At least some of them. You can forget the one about being neither a borrower nor a lender. It was said in jest. In imitation of your rather predictable and boring grandfather Polonius of Tulkarem in Palestine.

Remember: Love and learning. A yellow rose with dew covered leaves is worth a lifetime. Look at it and wonder.

And let all your tears for every letter of the alphabet wash your foundations clean to keep them strong.

Make sense of your life so that you can live forever. In trivia and in depth. Amen (and women, too).

Good night – or good morning to you both. May you look up and see each star pouring into you and touch the face of God. Each line of poetry. Each note of music. Each mystery of fiction. Each thrust of love. Should make your lives whole.

And what do you call a naked nun? I do not know what you would call a naked nun. But I know a lot more about beautiful Catholics. When I have read all the books in the world. Written all the books that I want to write. I think that I shall become a Catholic nun. Fully clothed.

I love you, my children.

8.50

Spectacularly deep sleep punctuated by ghosts at the door. Old old people walking in, staring at my sleeping body and walking out. Baby by the door smiling. Offering a boat ride. We head for the centre of the lake and I hold her to me. She speaks German and tells me about her parents. Her father refused to undress and a soldier shot him through the mouth. Her mother jumped in after him and was buried alive. And her brother survived and is killing Palestinians in Deir Yassin. A freedom fighter.

"Is this the same world that has your love in it?" she asks and I do not know what to say. I want to tell her that this is the Millennium. About the Internet. About the safety of our home, our bed, our poems. The boat capsizes and, coupled, we sink in and I see our net curtains stretch and move in the water. I can see her face clearly as if through a filter. We kiss as our bodies lunge at each other. What a sweet death. Unfrightening and voiding. It is 1947 and the world is black and white except for her little waistcoat: glowing orange as we die drowning.

I woke up happy and at peace. I went into the kitchen looking for Paula and found dead plants. I asked the stepstone if she wanted any shopping done. She said no.

"I will go to the Co-op. You have a good time. You know that the day I can't do my own commissions, I shall go aloft." And we laughed.

As I drove off, I saw her ninety years shuffle on the snow and felt proud of her selflessness and strong independence. And I hoped that my father took her out on the lake in 1929 and lunged his love into her young and beautiful body.

"You know," she said over lunch yesterday. "At night, when I can't sleep I watch my life's events move before my eyes. It is like a bad American movie. But I can make sense of it now."

Will I make sense of mine in 2038 when I am nearer her age? What horror! Alison will be 68 and Walid 65. It would be criminal. The cardinal duty of every good parent is to die at the earliest convenient opportunity before he messes his children's lives up. I hope that I have already died for my two.

I shall wade into the lake this morning. Until it freezes my very centre and lays me to an eternal rest. *In Switzerland they had brotherly love, they had 500 years of democracy and peace – and what did that produce? The cuckoo clock."*

My dear Harry, we may look like ants to you. Scurrying for survival. But each and every one of us carries a love eternal. A bond that creates giants. Imagine, Harry, if every word we uttered and every word we wrote could be seen. Each word according to its intent. Visible. The world will be obscured in a fog so black as to blind us. Occasionally, within the fog there will be a clear patch. That is where the "I love yous" and the screams of lovemaking will float: clear as fresh waters cascading on our lives. Always drowning our coupled bodies but never killing us.

1.30 pm

I am at the Touring earwigging on a conversation amongst six young Lebanese men. They are using portables in search of cars to buy. They appear menacingly handsome. They speak in Arabic in confident loud voices. One of them intersperses his sentences with immaculate French. They are discussing ways of buying cars without paying any tax. They have resolved the problem – a trifle dishonestly, I fear. Who said that Lebanon had no future? It is its past that I worry about.

I had lunch in a small ancient restaurant in Valengin. Odette, her brother Henri and his wife Madeleine. She is so beautiful – even at 70+ and after a long illness. Her blue eyes penetrate mine and I want to touch her face. This time I do so gently and she smiles at me. The stepladder is still under the impression that I have a soft spot for Isabelle the daughter; little knowing that it is the mother I admire and love so! Such ageless ineffable beauty. Paula's little eyes, body and cheeks.

We ate two and a half pain à beurre sizzling hot, a cream cornet, hot sweet black tea and coffee. A delicious meal. Henri spoke with the precision of pure intelligence, history and education. He invited me to spend the afternoon at the Sagne. Like a child refusing a hug for growing up, I refused politely. Swissticality is a state of liberation. A mind free and at ease with its own achievement.

In the restaurant, around the corner, sat Jean-Jacques, his wife and three of his grandchildren. Five of the seven ages of man. I went over and said hello and exchanged a few words. Odette waved to her younger brother. The three children ate politely and tended to their grandmother's needs and listened to their grandfather's stories.

And we all ate separately.

This is Switzerland's success: the Swiss have managed to bypass the oppressiveness of family relationships. They leave each other alone whilst uniting for the common good and in times of need. The only people in the world where the word community is seemingly attractive.

Yet this family has achieved continuity with progressive success in every single generation. No wonder the Swiss run finishing schools.

Henri spoke of Sophie's experience of English education. He had visited her with Madeleine. They loved London's history and its architecture. Henri could not understand how the English ever learnt anything. A people empty of curiosity, culture or ambition. He described England as a society of oppressive hypocrisy and intellectual dishonesty.

"These are a people without a national conscience. A tribal mentality where the old dominate and the young rebel. A nation of drunks," he added sipping his third or fourth glass of wine. I laughed and told him that I loved the British live and let live philosophy. It suited me. So I got a lecture on the necessity of solid educational foundations before the choices of liberty. I told him not to speak to the converted for I agreed. But that I still loved the idea of England.

"Ah, une idèe. Ideas soon dissipate and new fashions take over, old fellow."

I suddenly felt tired. Very tired. Without a structure there is nothing.

I believe now that I am beginning to suffer the alertness of coffee poisoning. I have had over twenty large black coffees since this morning. A feeling of nausea envelops my whole being.

And I am feeling tired with a heavy heart. One Lebanese left. He has an inordinately large head, a huge wide brow and ineffably feminine hands. A very young and loud blonde has joined him. Her favourite word appears to be the Swiss verb of "enmerder" – "you're shitting me".

I swap glasses in order better to observe.

Not my type. Little womanhood. But definitely what the common sheep would call a staggering beauty with a slim body, small breasts, dishevelled hair and gleaming teeth.

Not an ounce of healthy fat on her mortal coil.

He speaks wonderful French and makes her laugh with his stories. What storytellers we have become. The very history of our lives is an incessant fiction.

I am so tired. Tired beyond and chance of redemption. My chest feels heavy and oppressed.

Tomorrow I shall go to Guèvaux and look for ways to balm my children's hurt. I have that ancient duty of pouring balm. Even if too late.

Tired. To death for now.

5.20 pm

Words are for fiction. *Words, words, words.*

Action is for life.

Yet my words weigh heavily on others' actions. And their actions destroy my fiction.

My words. My children.

Just spent a delightful two hours reading in stepcorpse's company. She told me that one eye was gone but that the other was sufficient for "learning with".

You will have more life in you when you are dead than most living dead that I know.

"One must always be busy – being curious."

Right on. Cool. Yeah.

And may I add, mon cher corpse, that ignorance is a mule: obstinate, self-opinionated with a wonderfully sexy way of shitting while still walking. I have tried it by the river of blood and under the mountain of milk.

10.00 pm

You people have no eye for fiction. The fantastical linked with the mundane. To create tonight. Snow fluttering slowly; turning Neuchâtel sparkling white. When I saw it through the little window I had to rush into it and watch. *Death of a Salesman* could wait. Sorry Arthur. At least you got to love Marilyn Monroe. How was it for you? Did the ground shake un tout petit peu. Silence is probably best. For it would be impossible to describe one snowflake and pretend to know them all.

"I would've thought you'd gone off with one of the girls at the Touring." Why was it so hurtful? Even as a tasteless joke it shows a fear. A readiness for betrayal. A betrayal that will never ever happen. I have grown so happily securely accustomed to receiving permission. It makes me so yours. Completely and utterly. I wish it could be accepted with a smiling trust. Everlastingly. How I hate the effect that alcohol has on you. I am almost jealous of your dependency. For when they are all gone – and gone they will all be one and everyone, there will still be me. Devoted;

seeking love everlasting. Like a faithful dog. An old pipe –

favourite by now. A special armchair. Loving you. Accept.

Enjoy.

I can wait.

I love your very being – Paula.

25.01

1.00 am

Explicatory.

Genesis.

Exegesis.

In the beginning was the *litel bok* and the pocket full of pens. Then there was void. And the word was written. And it was good. The word was good.

All will be well. All manner of things will be well.

12.08 pm

I am in Guèvaux. Standing on the balcony. I have never experienced such cold. Piercing ice, in a variety of shapes hangs from trees, stones and metal. I break one and let it melt in my hand. I am beyond pain. The cold has anaesthetised my whole being and I can feel nothing. I have walked long.

The snow has come. Writing is very hard. I can not feel the pen. The cold has washed the memories away. For the first time I can understand how creative physics works.

I am home – for now. And I can not explain.

I need to calm down and cry less. No tears though.

2.00 pm

Nothing but warmth, peace and ahistoricity.

Albert Einstein joined me for tea. In faltering English, he spoke of Murten high street. Described how the tower would bend – actually bend – inwards as we travelled by at the speed of light. I held the teabag by the string and it rotated heavily – endlessly.

"And that?" I asked him pointing to the teabag.

"Oooh! Perpetual mo-tion. Voilà!"

That is what has happened to my love. Relativity gone haywire for now. And there is nothing that I can do about it as it stands.

I got up, went to a public phone and called 118. Soon I saw the flashing lights of the LAPD.

They took Albert away. The Swiss were furious.

"We're in the business of making money. You, les Américains, are dollar worshippers. So, what's the difference? We stole Jewish money. You steal everybody else's money."

Albert was incarcerated by the judge for being sane in an insane world.

They told me that there is a bed for me in his cell whenever I wanted it. I declined the offer and took up writing a new monograph: *"The Physics of Poetry: Special Theory of Word Relativity"*. Very difficult concept to explain. The formula is ridiculously simplistic: like all works of genius.

$$E = MC^2$$

Where E is the creative energy, M the overall mass of each word and C the speed of night. The squared is to make sure doubly sure. Divide if you will. This is creative physics.

Let me explain further.

Suppose you are walking upstairs to visit your stepmother of ninety. You observe a mat with a black cat on it. The image sticks. It starts its work. You have passed this way a hundred times before. A thousand.

At each passage you were someone else. Time sees to that. Once, in the sixties, you passed it and were full of Fatimah, her torn vagina and your anger. Thirty years later you are on the phone. You hear shouting in the background. Some woman is shouting, "Bosnia will be Muslim". You recognize the angry voice. It is new Fatimah.

A total of 100 words. A short narrative. Nothing in it, really.

That is where the equation comes in. To make order of embellishment.

Piazza della Repubblica

Florence

Dinner at Paszkowski in the Piazza della Repubblica was always perfect. The food was superb. The wine just right. The bread perfectly Italian - with so much more history in it than being mere cooked dough.

Frank sat in the customary corner as if he had lived in Florence all his life. Within minutes of arriving, Chameleon like, he had melded into Florence's daily life like a native. In fact, worse. Already a few hours in Florence, he had sung 'se vuol ballare signor Contino' to a bemused rank of bored taxi drivers. They applauded him with great Italian enthusiasm that always included a touch of irony somewhere deeprooted in all Italians did or said. He had then recited a few lines by Dante to a few peaceful old men sitting by the River Arno. They had listened politely, nodded amicably and smiled - just as if acknowledging that the accented massacre of Italy's greatest lines of poetry were too much to handle, even at such an advanced age.

Maybe they did not hear the dire warning to hypocrites calling themselves Christian whilst thinking evil thoughts of others.

"Guai a voi, anime prave:
non isperate mai veder lo cielo..."

Indeed, they shall never see heaven. Not with impurities in their so-called Christian hearts.

Frank's eyes wondered around the restaurant, as always, starting in one corner and making a circular journey of private stories.

To his left sat three women. The youngest was clad in relatively little and looked satisfied with herself. Beside her sat an older and, by far much prettier, woman who made a pretence of listening. Opposite the loosely clad woman sat a slightly older woman looking very bored. Initially, Frank watched the youngest woman because every time she leant forward she exposed the top half of her small bottom. But her gormless face, anorexic body and silly voice soon caused him to lose interest and switch his attention to the slightly older woman. Her bored look was interesting. She appeared to be there on sufferance and to resent it somewhat. She caught Frank's eye and smiled with a virtually imperceptible movement of her head inviting him to deal. He decided that he did not like her and moved his eyes to the oldest. She was a beautiful and rather full woman. Her intelligent eyes had a store of deep knowledge and understanding of men and their weaknesses. She caught Frank's eyes and smiled. She bent forward to give him a fleeting glance of two magnificent breasts. He immediately found himself getting interested. He stared at her awhile and then tried hard to hear the three women's conversation.

From the little Italian he had, he was able to work out that the oldest beauty was the boss. The bored one was the young one's mentor. And the youngest one was on her first outing. The boss explained that all the youngest one had to do was listen to the man, smile at him and excite him a little. He was paying for her company. No, there was no payment for sex. The young woman stood up, lifted her top to show her back, twirled around and was praised by the other two. She then sat down and looked worried. The mentor caught Frank's eye and smiled again, carrying the smile on to the youngest one, whose cheek she stroked reassuring her that she would be all right. Frank could not help but admire her style. The younger woman asked what she should do if the man pushed a bit. The older beauty told her to phone her and pass the phone onto the man. The mentor suggested that she could always relieve him with her hand to calm him down. The youngest one looked a little frightened. The mentor laughed, stroked her cheek again and told her to get used to men because she will be having them inside her regularly sooner than she thought. The beauty glared at the mentor and gently stroked the youngest girl's hand.

Frank looked away to the next table. A young man sat bolt upright staring through very dark glasses. His shirt was starched white and perfectly ironed. His trousers had a crease that was as sharp as a knife. His belt gleamed in the artificial light and his little shoes were mirror like in their polished perfection. He ate with great deliberation as if he were in the presence of royalty. He dialled a number on his mobile and waited impassively. Clearly, he was asked to leave a message. He left one saying, "I miss you honey. I hate being here alone without you. Call me please. I love you." Frank's heart went out to him. He had judged him to be somewhat stodgy when, in fact, he was a lonely man away from his beloved.

Frank felt ineffably lonely as he had done all his life. The woman sitting beside him looked at him affectionately but he seemed to ignore her. He was clearly one of those men happiest in his own company. She said something and he responded absently as his eyes roamed around the few tables around him starting again with the three women, moving on to the upright man on his own and then resting on a third table made up of a father, a mother, a son and a daughter. The father looked a little apprehensive. The mother kept adjusting her daughter's dress. They were a Lebanese family somewhat ill at ease in another country. The father looked somewhat severe but defeated. His wife sported a spectacularly unattractive face replicated twice by their two children. The father spoke but no one listened.

Occasionally, he dived into his briefcase earnestly in search of something that he never seemed to find, or, if found, to produce.

A fourth table had three Americans having a very loud discussion in that strongly nasal twang that appeared to demand the world's attention. They were discussing American foreign policy. One of them, speaking in a supremely loud voice, intoned somewhat stentoriously, "Why do they hate us so?" an echo of President Bush's famous question after the collapse of the Twin Towers in New York.

Frank listened attentively, bending his body forward.

"Why do they hate us so?" asked the stentorian American again.

"Viet Nam!" shouted Frank.

The three Americans looked at him in some shock at having received a response.

"Korea!" added Frank. "Afghanistan! Iraq! Palestine! Mexico!"

"Beirut!" shouted the defeated Lebanese.

"Sicily!" shouted the eldest beauty.

"But," started the American.

"But me no buts, sir. Yours is a nation with so much to commend it. But your double standards in foreign policy are what makes so many hate you so..." explained Frank.

"But, sir, we are the land of the free. We have the First Amendment..."

"Yes. Free to do and say whatever you want. Free even to burn other faiths' holy books. But if anybody dares criticise you or your abominable allies, the Israelis, they are terrorists..."

"That's right," said the Lebanese woman with the repellent aspect.

The three Americans looked a little embarrassed. They nodded and smiled politely.

"But we also love you," added Frank in a conciliatory tone. "Because we ape everything that you do. We crave to live like you. To be rich and powerful like you. To be free like you. All of us."

"Where do you come from sir?"

"Britain, sir."

"You too are free," argued stentorian.

"Yes, free as long as we are Christian. Free as long as we are white. Free as long as we believe in an archaic Monarchy. Free as long as we do what we're told... Come to think of it," reconsidered Frank. "We are like you Americans..."

The three Americans laughed. The Lebanese family clapped. The three women smiled and Beauty got up, walked over to Frank, held his face in her hands and planted a kiss on his cheek.

"Grazie!" He said.

"Prego," she replied as she walked back to her table.

Dinner arrived. Frank helped Joan to some salad, tucked his serviette under his chin and fell to with considerable gusto. He clearly enjoyed his meal as could be heard in the occasional appreciative grunt.

"You wait till I get you back into our room," said Joan.

Frank stopped eating, looked up with considerable outrage at being interrupted in his Dionysesian debauchery just to discuss something as mundane as sex. What had sex in comparison to good food?

Joan took her Blackberry out, took a picture and started writing a message. A few minutes later, Frank received a message.

"Fancy those in your face mister?" was written underneath a photograph of an ample cleavage which he recognised immediately as Joan's.

The next message read, "I shall lick you all over later and then I shall suck you till you scream!"

He looked up at Joan and she returned his look with a mischievous smile. He wondered if she had had too much wine.

She put her hand up to her mouth and moved sideways pushing her tongue into her cheek with every imagined thrust.

Dinner over, Frank suggested a walk. They stepped into the Piazza della Repubblica and walked towards The Uffizi. They arrived amidst its balustrades and walked slowly enjoying the statues. Frank turned back on his heels and went back to the Palazzo Vechio and stood in front of David's statue. He stared at the angular face, muscular arms and beautiful body with his eye stopping at the limp penis so high above him. For years he had loved this statue and found its penis exciting. He used to joke that David was the only man he could be with because he was so lovely.

Joan joined him. She entwined her arm into his and stared up at David.

"So real. He looks as if he would move if you touched him. Take it in your hand and he might get excited."

"He is magnificent. Well done Michaelangelo. What great talent. I love David," said Frank.

"Yes. But not what he stands for," answered Joan. "The ugly Judeo-Christian tradition of Old Testament cruelty, hypocrisy and vindictiveness. That ugly book epitomises all the horrors being perpetrated this very minute on poor Palestinians..."

"Not now," said Frank abruptly. "Don't spoil all of this beauty with disgusting Old Testament vicious nonsense... Please. We're on holiday."

"Sorry," said Joan. "Kiss me."

Frank turned her around to face him. He held her in his arms and kissed her.

She responded and moaned quietly.

She pushed herself forward so that their loins touched.

"You're not stiff..." she whispered.

"Just tired my dear," he replied.

Her hand went down and clutched his manhood. She massaged it gently.

"We'll soon have it ready for action. I want you inside me tonight. It's been so long..."

They walked on and emerged by the Arno. They walked across the Ponte Vecchio looking into the various jewellers' windows. As they came towards the last shop, Frank took Joan's hand and pulled her into the shop.

"I would like the cameo in the gold setting, please."

The woman behind the counter answered in a nasal American voice. She produced the tray and placed it on the counter. Frank pointed out the wanted article.

The woman gave him the price and he looked politely chockod ac ho agrood to buy it.

As they walked out of the shop, Joan held on to him and whispered, "Thank you, darling".

They walked up the Via Romana for a long time. Arriving at Piazza della Calza, Frank realised that it was past midnight and headed back towards the Piazza della Repubblica.

They stopped and had a drink before resuming their tired walk towards the Savoy Hotel. Passing David, Frank looked up at him and fancied that he was mocking the couple walking by. David's penis looked a lot bigger because of the various directional lights casting shadows everywhere.

As they arrived in their room, Frank filled the bath with very hot water. He got in and lay with the water up to his neck.

Joan knelt by the bath.

"You're a handsome bugger. Not bad for an old man. Look at that beauty..." She pointed to his floating penis. "I'm having you tonight. You're gonna have me till I scream enough..."

"All right, old girl..."

Joan got up, washed herself at the sink and went to bed. He could see her lying back quietly. She waved to him.

He closed his eyes and tried hard to remember.

"You have my blessing..."

He played one of his internal films and watched quietly.

Emerging from the bath, he dried himself and walked towards the bed.

Tentatively, he sat beside her recumbent form.

She was fast asleep - exhausted by the long walk.

Quietly, he got up, dressed and left the room.

He went downstairs and sat in the lounge. He ordered a drink. In the corner sat a man and a woman. It took him some time to get used to the semi darkness and realise that the woman was the youngest of the three at Paszkowski's. The man was sitting in the corner with his head thrown slightly back. The young woman's hand was moving regularly up and down where his manhood was. She was whispering something. The man groaned softly and raised his midrift. Her hand stopped moving as her other hand picked a serviette up. She wiped her hand and then placed the serviette in his crotch.

Frank froze for fear of being discovered. The man adjusted his trousers and got up. He bent down and whispered something to the young woman. She took the money that he gave her. He left without looking back.

She sat awhile staring ahead of her. She took out her mobile and dialled a number. She spoke into the set quietly.

"I had to..." Frank heard her say. She added, "He was kind... Five hundred. Can I go home for the night. I'll be back tomorrow. Yes, Lina, I'll bring the money first... Yes ma'am."

She got up and suddenly noticed Frank.

He smiled. She approached him.

"Buona sera, signore."

"Buona sera, signora." he replied.

He looked at her and noticed her cheeks gleaming with two perfect tears.

He got up, walked towards her, hugged her gently and whispered, "Bene. Bene."

She nodded smiling.

She walked out of the hotel. Frank took the lift to the fifth floor.

He slept fitfully.

He woke up early, showered and sat by the window looking out at the Duomo.

Joan woke up soon after and, after breakfast, they visited the crypts in the Campanila di Giotto.

They admired the paintings reproduced for tourists. They looked at the rather tacky memorabilia.

Joan picked up a small icon that folded such that two little wooden doors closed it in. The central piece had a rather angular Virgin Mary with a somewhat capricious looking Baby Jesus. The two doors had similar painted faces.

"Ugly looking thing..." murmured Frank.

"No. No." Joan spoke softly but urgently. "I love it..."

Frank looked at her and at the small icon. He turned again with an expression of real disgust.

Joan looked like a child, her eyes open wide with a tear sitting on a lid waiting for gravity to do its job.

Frank smiled, opened the icon and said, rather unconvincingly, "It would look beautiful on your desk love... Here, look at those posters and choose us one for the kitchen."

Joan turned her back and starting flicking through the posters as the tear trickled down her cheek. She flicked it off with an impatient gesture of her hand.

Frank joined her, took her arm and they climbed up the steep steps.

As they sat in their usual seats at Paszkowski, Frank produced a little gift wrapped objoot and gavo it to Joan.

She opened it, looked at the icon and burst into tears.

He held her in his arms and gently patted her shoulders.

They placed the icon in front of them, had dark hot chocolate and chatted quietly about the rest of their day.